Out of the Park

by Andrew Einspruch

EDUCATORS PUBLISHING SERVICE
Cambridge and Toronto

© 2008 by Educators Publishing Service, a division of School Specialty Publishing, a member of the School Specialty Family

Series Authors: Kay Kovalevs and Alison Dewsbury
Commissioning Editors: Rachel Elliott, Tom Beran, Lynn Robbins, and Laura Woollett
Text by Andrew Einspruch
Illustrated by Paul Konye
Edited by Gemma Smith
Text designed by Miranda Costa
Cover designed by Jenny Jones
Cover photographs: Shutterstock Photos

Making Connections® developed by Educators Publishing Service, a division of School Specialty Publishing, and Pearson Education Australia, a division of Pearson Australia Group Pty Ltd

ISBN 978 0 8388 3352 0

1 2 3 4 5 PEA 12 11 10 09 08

Printed in China.

Contents

Chapter 1
The Firebats

Min Su Kim held the bat. He was expecting the Mud Sox pitcher to throw a backdoor slider. The count was three balls and two strikes, and Min Su had been watching their pitcher all afternoon. "I'd better be right," thought Min Su. His team, the Firebats, was down by one run and it was the bottom of the ninth with two outs.

His best friend Luke edged away from first base, ready to run.

The Mud Sox pitcher wound up and let the ball fly. "There it is!" It took Min Su only a second to read the pitch. "Sometimes math is handy," he thought and hit the ball hard past the first baseman. As it bounced toward the right-field fence, Luke flew around the bases. He crossed home plate and scored the tying run. Min Su ran even faster, desperate to charge home with the winner. As the right fielder hurled the ball toward the infield, the Firebats' third base coach waved Min Su in. In a cloud of dust, Min Su slid over home plate. It was an inside-the-park home run! A fraction of a second later, the ball thudded into the catcher's mitt. Too late. Game over.

The Firebats were one game away from the playoffs.

"That was a fantastic hit," said Luke as he and Min Su walked home after the game. "It was like you knew that pitch was coming."

"I did, pretty much." Min Su shifted his bat from one shoulder to the other.

"Really?"

Min Su nodded. "For the whole game, when the count was three and two, the pitcher threw a backdoor slider around two-thirds of the time. But if you only looked at lefty hitters, on three and two, he threw a slider around ninety percent of the time."

"And you hit lefty."

Min Su nodded again. "Yup. Sometimes math is handy."

"You keep saying that. Today, I actually believe you."

Luke and Min Su reached the cement courtyard of the crowded apartment complex where their families lived.

"What are you going to do for our English assignment?" asked Min Su. Their English teacher had assigned a poetry project. The students had to choose a famous poem and write something about it. "I hate it when teachers say, 'Just be creative' and leave you to it."

"I'm thinking about writing an essay on Longfellow's 'The Midnight Ride of Paul Revere,'" said Luke. "What about you?"

"I was thinking about using 'Casey at the Bat,'" said Min Su as they waited for the elevator. "Maybe I could rewrite it from the point of view of the other team. I'd make the hero the pitcher who struck Casey out."

The elevator door dinged open. "Wow," said Luke, pressing the four and the eight. "You can work baseball into anything."

Three minutes later, Min Su was fumbling in his left pocket for his keys when his right pocket yelled, "Play ball! Batter up! Play ball! Batter up!" He fished out his cell phone and saw that it was his mother. "Hi, Uhmma [OO-mah]. What's up? I'm just outside the door."

"I'm at the hospital," said his mother. "It's your grandmother."

Min Su's stomach tightened. "What's happened to Halmoni [HAL-mon-ee]? She's not . . . you know?"

"No, no, no. Your Halmoni is like a steel statue. She's going to live forever."

Min Su could tell his mother was trying to be lighthearted, but she was clearly upset. "Sadly, she's now a steel statue with a crack in it. She had a fall. Halmoni was playing a board game at

Aunt Lee's. She slipped on a playing piece that had fallen on the floor and fractured her hip."

"Ouch! Will she be alright?"

"She's in surgery now."

Four hours later, Min Su and his mother watched his grandmother sleep. The carnations he'd brought stood in a vase, ready for Halmoni to see when she woke up. "Uhmma, Halmoni's going to be alright, isn't she?"

"The doctors say she should recover, but it will take time."

Something in his mother's voice was strained. Min Su could tell there was bad news mixed in with the good. "And?"

His mother idly stroked one of the leaves of the carnations, as if she were testing it for dust. "And? And it's all going to cost a lot of money. A lot more than we have."

"Don't we have insurance?"

"Not enough to cover all the bills. Not since your father died."

"Oh." Min Su's father had died in a factory accident the previous year. The loss was still raw, but the three of them were coping. Min Su lightly squeezed his mother's hand. "We'll work something out, Uhmma."

Chapter 2
Money Trouble

A few days later, Min Su stood next to a walker and held out a hand to his grandmother. "Please, Halmoni. The doctor said you should be moving around on your own now. Please can't you try again?"

"Doctors, phaw!" She tossed her Korean-language newspaper down on the bed. "For you, my baby, I will try again." Gingerly, she slid off the bed and balanced herself in the walker.

Meanwhile, Min Su's mother was working with a spreadsheet and a stack of bills. Suddenly, she closed the lid of her ancient laptop with a sharp clack and stomped to the kitchen. Uhmma stirred the vegetarian rice-cake soup she was making for dinner. Min Su and Halmoni slowly entered the kitchen. They took one look at Uhmma and could tell she was upset about something.

"What?" Uhmma said when she saw them staring at her. "What's going on?"

"What is going on is that you look sour-faced," said Halmoni. "It will spoil the soup."

"It's just . . ." For a moment, the only sound was her knife chopping white radish. "It's just that I can't make the numbers add up. The bills from the hospital are impossible to pay on top of everything else. I don't know how we're going to make it." She looked at Min Su. "Sweetie, I hate to ask you because I want you to focus on studying. But, maybe you could get some sort of job after school—just to help out."

Min Su threw the ball to Luke. The sky above the ball field was bright blue, and the two were warming up for practice. "I've got to find a job or something. We need the money. My mother is really worried."

The ball gave a soft "pop" as it settled into Luke's catcher's mitt. "Good luck. With things the way they are, you know, the economy and all, my older brother's been out of work for months." Luke chucked the ball back.

"Do you have ideas about where you could work?"

"I've been trying to figure out my options. It doesn't look like there are a lot of possibilities."

"You could always sling burgers at a fast-food joint."

Min Su caught Luke's next throw. He stood there, looking at his friend.

"Right," said Luke. "You're vegetarian. Cooking and serving up dead cows and chickens probably isn't going to work for you." He caught Min Su's throw, then balanced the ball on the back of his hand. "Remember that lemonade stand we had when we were seven?"

"Yeah. We made four dollars and thirty-seven cents. I think I'm going to have to do better than that." Min Su sighed. "You should see what the hospital charged for my grandmother's operation. Ouch."

Coach Planer gathered the Firebats into a huddle. "Okay, team. If we beat the Steamrollers on Friday, then we're in the playoffs. If we don't, then we're watching the playoffs from the bleachers. Now let's go out there and work hard."

Min Su wandered over to his shortstop position. He turned the job problem over in his mind. It had to be a job that paid a good amount of money. But what was a kid like him with no experience, no driver's license, and not much time going to do? Maybe he could create an online store. No one knows how old you are in cyberspace. But what could he sell? He had some old comic books. But they probably weren't worth enough to sell. Min Su pounded his fist into his glove. He dug his toe into the dirt. Uhmma needed the money soon. She was counting on him.

The batter hit a line drive that hopped past Min Su. Coach Planer's bellowing broke through his thoughts. "Hey, Min Su, that's the second ball you let get past you. Would our team captain care to join us for practice?"

"Sorry, Coach." Min Su pushed away his money worries and concentrated on keeping his eye on the ball.

Chapter 3
Doing the Math

Min Su parked his bike under a sign that said, "We Can Move It. Ask Inside." His Uncle Sung owned a moving company, which always seemed busy. It seemed like a reasonable job possibility.

Min Su knocked on the door of Uncle Sung's office and poked his head in. "Hey! Come in, Min Su. How's my nephew?"

"Hi, Uncle Sung. I'm good."

"Hit any home runs lately?"

"One or two. We're one game away from the playoffs."

"Good luck to you." Uncle Sung pointed to a threadbare chair that sat opposite his desk. "So, is this just a friendly visit? Does your mother need help with something?"

Min Su cleared his throat, surprised at how nervous he was. He decided a direct approach would be best. "I was wondering, Uncle Sung, if you might have a part-time job I could apply for. I'm strong and I would work hard."

Uncle Sung raised his eyebrows. "A job? Aren't you in school? Don't you play baseball, not to mention studying?"

"I was thinking on the weekend, when I have time." But even as he said it, he could see the "no" written on his uncle's face.

Uncle Sung grabbed an apple from his desk drawer and offered it to Min Su. When Min Su declined, Uncle Sung took a bite, giving himself a few moments before he answered. "Min Su, let me tell you something. When I was younger, I worked forty-eight hours per day, fourteen days a week. It practically killed me. When my heart started acting up, I knew I'd better make a change. Now, I work during the week and take weekends off to spend with my family. So does everyone else here. Besides, my movers start early and work all day all over the city, so an afternoon worker isn't going to work out."

Min Su listened to his uncle go on about the family for a few minutes before excusing himself. His uncle patted him on the back as Min Su walked out the door. "Good luck making the playoffs."

Min Su's mother and grandmother were arguing. Min Su could hear it even before he opened the front door. He listened quietly as they argued back and forth in Korean and English. It seemed to have something to do with his mother's boss.

"*You* talk to your mother," snapped Halmoni as Min Su dropped his backpack behind a chair. "She and the rest of the workers are letting those greedy bosses have their way."

Min Su looked at his mother's teary, red eyes. Her knuckles were white as she crushed a wet tissue.

"Uhmma? Are you okay?"

"I'm losing hours at work."

Halmoni angrily broke in, "Because those lousy bosses don't know how to run a business."

"The company isn't doing well," said Min Su's mother. "All of us on the assembly line agreed to work fewer hours rather than have some people lose their jobs."

"That seems honorable."

"Phaw!" spat Halmoni. "There is no honor in letting greedy bosses steal your money."

"Mother, please," said Uhmma. "That does not help."

Min Su's grandmother huffed off to her room as fast as her walker would take her.

Dinner was tense that night. Uhmma made pancakes from green peas, sticky rice powder, bean sprouts, and vegetables. It was usually a favorite, but it hardly made anyone smile.

After dinner, Min Su helped his mother do the dishes. He told her about his failed mission at Uncle Sung's.

"He was right. With everything I'm doing, I don't know how I'm supposed to fit in a job."

Min Su's mother handed him the last dish and folded her arms. She was careful not to get her blouse wet with the rubber gloves. "Perhaps your priorities need to change."

"My priorities?"

"Well, you can't give up school or stop doing homework."

"Obviously."

"But baseball . . ." Her voice trailed off.

"You want me to quit baseball?" Min Su gasped. "I'm the team captain! We're almost in the playoffs!"

His mother pulled off her rubber gloves and headed for her desk. "Well, I just don't know what to do." She picked up a stack of printed pages and handed them to him. "You're good at math. You make these add up."

Min Su looked down. It was their budget. There were a couple of numbers for income, and a much, much larger set of numbers showing all their expenses.

His mother left him looking at the sheets of paper. Her last words were, "I'm sure you'll do the right thing." Min Su had learned over the years that this normally translated as, "I'm sure you'll do what I've asked."

That night, Min Su sat in his room reworking "Casey at the Bat." He'd come up with a name for the team that played against the Mudville nine (the Atlantics) and a name for the pitcher who would strike out Casey (Rockman). He'd even written the first line: "The outlook was pretty rosy for the Atlantics nine that day." But then he got stuck.

Taking a break, he picked up his mother's budget pages. Their lives were hardly extravagant. They only occasionally got take-out or bought new clothes. It was hard to see where they could cut back. But everything was different now that Uhmma was working less. Min Su could see why worry lines seemed etched on his mother's face these days.

He did a quick calculation in his head. He thought about how much time he had for a job now, and how much more time he would have if he quit the Firebats. He was not likely to find a job that paid very much, so more hours would definitely make a difference.

Min Su found his mother in the kitchen making Halmoni a cup of green tea. He took a deep breath. "Okay, Uhmma. I'll do it."

"Do what?"

"Quit baseball."

"I knew you would do the right thing for your family."

"Yes, Uhmma. Give me one more game and I'll tell everyone."

Chapter 4
The Last Game

The last regular-season game saw the Firebats up against the Steamrollers, the team tied with them for second place in their division. Both teams expected it to be a tense slugfest, with the game going down to the wire.

Not this time. The Firebats brought home the division title with an easy win. The Steamrollers' pitching collapsed somewhere in the fifth inning and never recovered. Min Su played like it was his last game ever, batting in six runs and making out after out. He even hit a home run that flew out of the park. He should have been happy. But all Min Su could think about was how he was the one who'd be out of the park, once he quit the team.

Winning the game was the easy part. As he walked to the locker room after the game, Min Su was filled with dread. He swung his bat over his shoulder. Telling the team he was quitting would be really hard. Min Su expected his teammates to be disappointed or sad. Maybe they'd be angry.

What he didn't expect was laughter—gale-force laughter.

No one believed him. They just cracked up, saying, "Sure, right, whatever." Min Su tried to show his teammates that he was serious. But everyone only laughed harder.

"Good joke," said Coach Planer as he clapped Min Su on the shoulder and left the locker room.

"So, how did it go?" Min Su's mother looked up from ironing his grandmother's blouse.

"Good. We won. The team is in the playoffs."

His mother kept ironing. Finally, she prompted him. "Did you tell them about leaving the team?"

Min Su scanned the inside of the fridge so she couldn't read his face. "Yes, Uhmma. I told them."

More ironing. "And?"

"And they reacted more or less like you would expect."

Luke caught the ball Min Su had batted high in the air. They were practicing catching pop-ups. "So you're not even supposed to be here at practice?" He lobbed it high for Min Su to catch. "Sheesh. I'd hate to be you if your mom finds out. When she goes into Scary Mom mode, the sun freezes and the moon hides."

The ball thudded on the ground next to Min Su. "Tell me about it." He picked it up and batted it high again. "I'm supposed to be job hunting."

"What are you going to tell her?" Luke leapt for the ball, catching it firmly in his glove.

"The truth," said Min Su. "That I didn't find any work today."

"That's not the whole truth." Luke took off his catcher's mask and looked his friend straight in the eye. "Don't you think your mother's radar will pick that up a mile away?"

"She's working the late shift this week. I don't think it's going to be a problem yet."

In the cafeteria, Min Su sipped his bean curd and miso soup. He liked its hot pepper paste. It distracted him from the classified ads in the local paper, where he was looking for anything remotely like a suitable job. He wondered if there were any ads seeking underage, part-time workers with no experience. And who wouldn't work at a fast-food restaurant on principle. And who needed to earn a lot more than minimum wage. There didn't seem to be any. He wasn't exactly surprised.

Luke dropped into the chair next to Min Su. "Your grandmother's soup?" Min Su nodded. "Give me a sip." Min Su slid over the plastic container. "Yow, that's hot! Fantastic!" Luke motioned for Min Su's water and took a gulp.

He pointed at Min Su's newspaper. "You know, my brother's still trying to find a job. But he doesn't even look at those ads. He keeps saying that most of the jobs come from who you know, not from ads. Maybe you need to network or something."

Min Su nodded. "The 'or something' is the tricky part." He reached for the rest of his soup. "So what did Coach say when I missed practice yesterday?"

"I covered for you. I said you had the flu or something, but that it was getting better, and you'd be back tomorrow. I'm not sure he believed me, but he didn't push it."

"Right. Thanks, I think. So did you finish the geometry assignment?"

Luke rolled his eyes. "You know me and math. I'm not like you! I'd rather sleep on a bed of sharp number-two pencils than figure out the area of a triangle."

"Well, let me know if you need a hand."

Chapter 5
The Light Bulb

Eight very long days crept by. Min Su snuck off to practice when he thought he could get away with it. Or he missed practice when he thought he could get away with it. On those afternoons, he walked around his neighborhood looking for work. He picked up an odd job digging a trench down an alleyway, which left his shoulder so sore he could barely throw a ball from second base to home. At another odd job, he sorted rotten cabbages from fresh ones.

Min Su stacked the pathetic pile of money he'd managed to collect during the week on the kitchen table. It hardly felt like it had been worth the stress and effort. It hadn't amounted to much more than half a trip to the grocery store.

There was a muffled jangle of keys and his mother opened the front door. She seemed more tired than usual. Halmoni shuffled in behind her and went straight to her room. Neither of them greeted him.

"Hi, Uhmma."

His mother just looked at him and went to the kitchen.

Min Su let the silence hang for five minutes to see if Uhmma would say anything. She didn't.

"What's up, Uhmma?"

"What's up? What's up is that I had a call today from your baseball coach." Min Su's stomach felt like it had just been hit by a sharp line drive. "He asked me about your health. Apparently, you have missed a practice or two and your friend Luke had said something about the flu."

"Uhmma . . ."

"You told me you quit the team. You said you were looking for a job. I have a son who lies to his mother."

"But . . ."

"I suggest you leave the room." It was not her usual Scary Mom routine with all the yelling and theatrics. It was sadder, quieter, and much more effective.

Min Su went to his bedroom and did not dare come out for dinner. The next morning, his small pile of earnings lay where he had left it—untouched, unnoticed, and unacceptable.

Min Su sat in the library and finished his version of "Casey at the Bat," which he called "Rockman on the Mound." In his mind, he relived that morning's practice when he had told the team that he'd be missing the playoffs. This time he had made sure they believed him.

Next to him, Luke sweated over his geometry assignment. "Ugh! I can never remember how to find the area of a circle."

"Apple pie are square," said Min Su, hardly realizing he'd spoken out loud.

"Huh? Apple pies are round."

"No, 'apple pie are square' is the formula. Area equals pi times the radius squared. $A = \pi r^2$. That's how I remember the area of a circle." Min Su continued to explain. Luke looked at his friend with a mixture of wonder and awe.

"I get it! I actually get it!" said Luke. Min Su could practically see the huge light bulb shining over Luke's head. "Geez, people would pay for that kind of thing."

And that's when the light bulb went on over Min Su's head, too.

Chapter 6
Tutor Workshop

Min Su stood outside the door to
Tutor Workshop. It was the fanciest
after-school tutoring service in the
area. Of all the tutoring companies
he'd visited that day, it had the nicest
furniture and the most people coming in
and out. Most importantly, it charged
the highest prices. Min Su pulled down
the cuffs on his slightly-too-small suit

jacket, and walked inside.

The receptionist flashed a well-practiced, but welcoming smile. "Good afternoon and welcome to Tutor Workshop. How can we help you?"

Min Su cleared his throat softly. "Do you happen to need a math tutor?"

The receptionist showed him to the director's office. "Mr. Taylor, this young man is looking for a job."

Mr. Taylor turned out to be a math buff himself. Within minutes of meeting each other, he and Min Su were trading math memory tips. Half an hour later, Min Su had a part-time job tutoring math students. Best of all, he would earn around six times more per hour than he would at a fast-food restaurant or sorting cabbages. It meant he could work fewer hours, make more money, and still have time for the thing he loved—baseball.

"Sometimes math is handy," Min Su thought to himself. He jumped on his bike and raced toward the baseball field. In forty minutes, the Firebats would play their first playoff game. He calculated that he'd make it with five minutes to spare.